In Memory of
Marsali Catriona

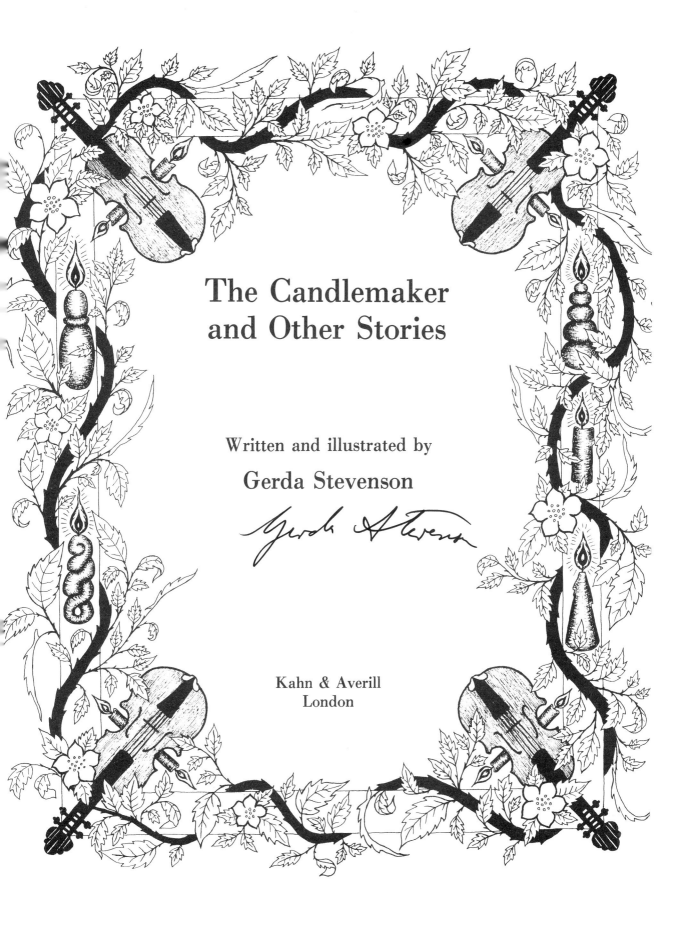

The Candlemaker and Other Stories

Written and illustrated by

Gerda Stevenson

Kahn & Averill
London

First published in 1987 by Kahn & Averill
Copyright stories and illustrations © 1987 by Gerda Stevenson

British Library Cataloguing in Publication Data

Stevenson, Gerda
    The candlemaker and other stories.
    I. Title
    823'.914[J]   PZ7

ISBN 0-900707-86-0

Set in 13 on 14pt Bodoni by Mathematical Composition Setters Ltd, Ivy Street, Salisbury.

The Rose's Warning
The Candlemaker
Princess Sorroway-over-the-Sea

The Rose's Warning

NCE UPON a time, in a far away country, there was a rose. She grew on top of a mountain, overlooking a lake. Her first petals blossomed on Midsummer Day, and so she became enchanted.

From her high mountain home she watched over the valley below. By day, she liked to see clouds sailing across the mirror of the lake's surface; at night it seemed to her the stars shone both in the sky and on earth.

But most of all, she loved to watch the fisher lad, who lived at the foot of the mountain. Each day at dawn she saw him open the door of his house. The morning light gleamed on his head of golden curls as he tramped over the grass to the lake's shore. There he climbed into a small boat. When he reached the middle of the lake he stopped rowing and pulled in the oars. From under his seat he took out a fishing rod and skilfully cast the line into the water, making a soft 'plip', that could be heard right across the lake. When the sun had risen, he returned to his cottage with a large sack full of fresh fish ready to take to market.

Each day the rose watched all this. The valley was peaceful and the fisher lad happy in his work. And yet, sometimes she thought the valley was too silent. She longed to hear children's voices echoing through the mountains.

One morning she awoke to find that her stem was bent, her flower almost touching the ground. A heavy weight held her down, and her leaves were moist, even though the sun was shining. Water was flowing from her, and she could hear a mournful weeping.

"Perhaps an insect is trapped inside me," she thought, and carefully unfolded each delicate petal. There, in her centre, lay a dewdrop.

"Why are you weeping?" asked the rose.

"I am weeping," sobbed the dewdrop, "because I want to be a girl. For many mornings I have lain in your petals, and watched the lad fishing in the lake. I love him, but cannot even speak to him, for I am only a dewdrop."

"But, you are fortunate," replied the rose, "and should be contented; mortals do not live long and in their short lives there is great sadness."

"No, you don't understand," wept the dewdrop. "I can never be happy again."

The rose could not bear to see her friend distressed. She wished she could do something to help. Remembering her powers, she said, "I am enchanted. I can transform you into a mortal on one condition: you must never weep. Your tears shall still be dew, and if you weep, you will become a drop of rainwater that will fall into the lake below and disappear forever."

The dewdrop smiled. Now that her sorrow had gone she was no longer heavy, and the rose stood up straight in the sunshine.

"I shall be as happy as the happiest mortal on earth," laughed the dewdrop.

"How happy will that be?" the rose wondered.

Then she sprinkled her pollen over the dewdrop and whispered a spell in strange words. A cloud of golden dust drifted up from the petals, and gathered itself into the shape of a girl. A river of yellow hair swept down her back. Her skin was as soft as mountain moss, and her eyes were two deep pools of dew. She knelt to kiss the rose in gratitude, and ran down the mountainside. For the first time she felt the touch of the earth beneath her feet as they bore her swiftly into the world of mortals.

The sun was still low in the sky. The lad was fishing out on the lake as usual, but the girl did not dare to call him.

"I must find somewhere to live," she decided. Her eyes surveyed the shores of the lake and rested on a stone building, partly concealed by a wood of fir trees.

"Perhaps someone living there will give me work to do and a bed to sleep in," she thought.

But on reaching the wood she suddenly felt afraid and stopped. Peering through the gloomy light enclosed by the dark green firs, she could just make out two windows set deep into the walls of the cottage. The glass was covered in dust and spiders' webs. The door stood ajar, and a few scraggy hens clucked in a rickety wooden pen. It seemed to her this must be the loneliest place in all the world, and she wondered who could possibly live in such solitude. Still afraid, but overcome by curiosity, she tiptoed up the garden path. Weeds brushed her ankles, and wild flowers glanced at her from behind pebbles; it must have been many days since human feet had stepped that way.

She tapped on the door, but caught her breath sharply as the sound shattered the eerie stillness. Nothing stirred within the cottage. She dared not knock again, but pushed the door open a little further. Its rusty hinges creaked and she hardly breathed as she crept over the threshold.

She found herself in a small dim room, furnished with a couple of chairs next to a large fireplace. An empty kettle sat on the hob, and among charred wood and cold ashes, which lay sleeping in the grate, she discovered a piece of paper. It was yellow and burnt at the edges, with the words "Gone away" scrawled over it. Perhaps it had fallen from the mantlepiece.

"Indeed, this house is one of sorrow," thought the girl, remembering the rose's warning.

But she set to
work. She scrubbed the
floor, cleaned the windows
and aired the musty blankets
crumpled on the old box bed.
She lit a fire, and soon the kettle was whistling on the hob. She fed the
hens with meal from a sack she found under the kitchen sink. The
hungry creatures clucked with pleasure when they saw her open the
gate of their pen, carrying a bucket of delicious brown meal under her
arm. After a few days they began to lay large speckled eggs.

The girl had not forgotten her beloved fisher lad. Every morning she awoke before dawn and walked along the shore to his cottage. Not once did she knock on the door, but merely placed a box of eggs on the step. Then she would run away, disappearing among the fir trees just in time to see him open the door, take the box inside and set off to fish in the lake.

It puzzled the fisher lad to find these eggs on his doorstep each day. He had noticed smoke rising from the cottage in the forest, and guessed they might be a gift from someone living there. He determined to find out for certain, so one morning he got up earlier than usual and hid behind his house.

When the girl bent down to put her gift on the step, he crept from his hiding place. Seeing the silhouetted figure crouched in the dark, he opened his lips to speak, but stood dumbfounded as the girl turned towards him. The shaft of light from his lantern had fallen across her face. He fell in love with her at once, and before the sun had risen to greet the day they had agreed to share their lives with one another.

They lived in her cottage by the fir trees. Before long, two children were born to them, a boy and a girl. When they were old enough they went fishing with their father; afterwards, while he went to market, they helped their mother in the garden, feeding the hens, collecting eggs and tending the vegetables.

"Wait until daylight," she said to her husband, one day as he and the children set out to fish.

"I'll be late for market if I wait," he replied.

It was dark, and the full moon cast a cold blue light over the lake's ruffled surface. The father took up the oars. A sudden gust of wind blew out the lantern flame, just as the moon disappeared behind a billowing cloud. Darkness surrounded them.

"Father," asked the little girl, "why is it so windy, and why is the light of the moon so strange?"

"Indeed it is strange," agreed her father, still rowing. "And that is because last night was Midwinter, the longest night in the year, when evil spirits of the underworld are about. Although it is morning, darkness is still here, and they won't return to the underworld until daylight. But you mustn't be afraid; we are safe so long as we stay in the middle of the lake."

But without a light to show the way, he had rowed beyond the middle of the lake, and the boat was now nearing the opposite shore, where

He fell in love with her
~ at once ~

no-one dared venture; for there, unknown spirits were thought to inhabit the deep waters. A weird moaning was heard and the children moved closer together, huddled in each other's arms.

"Don't be afraid," their father reassured them. "It's only the wind."
Suddenly the boat began to tip, until one side was touching the water. Without a sound it turned right over and the father and his children slipped quietly into the lake.

At home the mother was stirring a pot of porridge. The rising steam covered her face in tiny droplets. Every few moments she glanced over her shoulder to the window. A worried frown furrowed her brow. It was daylight and her husband and children had not returned. She laid down the spoon, reached for her shawl and opened the door.

"Ah, there's the boat on the other side of the lake," she sighed with relief. But looking again she noticed that there was no-one in it. She rushed down to the shore and peered across the lake. The boat was upturned.

"My husband and children drowned!"

Grief-stricken, she fell to the ground. Tears brimmed in her eyes, but suddenly she recalled the rose's warning.

"No, I mustn't weep. In spite of everything, I must not weep."

And just in time she stopped the tears from falling. But her sorrow was deep and in her heart she wept.

She lived alone. Often she thought of the day she found the cottage amid the dark firs. It seemed so desolate with cobwebs and dust and cold ashes. She had thought it the saddest place in all the world then.

It was now she knew the true meaning of sorrow. Her loved ones were gone and she felt like a ghost in a house full of memories. There stood the three beds, two small ones and a big one, and the four chairs around the table. Yes, the rose was right, the life of a mortal was sad and hard to bear. Many times her eyes filled with tears, but always she remembered the solemn words of the rose, and restrained her sorrow.

Three years passed, then four and five.

One morning, long after the disappearance of her husband and children, she was taking a walk by the lake. The sun glimmered above the blue mountain ridge and tinged the sky with rose and violet. A curtain of mist, hanging between lake and shore, was slowly drawn apart by the invisible fingers of dawn. As she gazed long and thoughtfully, the form of a rowing boat appeared on the other side of the lake. It rocked gently, and three people were sitting in it. Their bodies were bent and old. Their hair was white as foam. Two of them had long flowing beards. Now they seemed to change, their bodies straightened, their hair turned to gold, and the beards of the two old men disappeared.

~ Their bodies were bent and old ~

A man and two children were rowing towards her.

"My husband and children!" she cried. "They've come back to me! They've come back!"

Sobbing for joy, tears flowing down her cheeks, she rushed into the water to meet the boat. Deeper and deeper into the water she waded, until the lake's bed slipped from her feet. Her tears seemed to give her strength as she swam far out to meet her loved ones. She saw the children waving and her husband calling. He was rowing towards her with all his might. She almost touched the oars.

But suddenly her strength ebbed and the waves swept her back. Her voice had lost its sound, and as her flesh dissolved, a pale vapour floated up from the lake's surface. Dancing in the blue, it climbed higher and higher. When at last it disappeared, a raindrop fell into the lake.

The rose had warned her that a mortal's life is full of sorrow, and that if she wept, she would die, dissolving into the lake forever.

But the rose had never guessed the girl would die of joy.

The Candlemaker

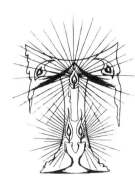

HERE ONCE was a sad old man. He was a candle-maker, and a very good one too. No-one could make such beautiful candles — candles of all shapes and sizes, twisting and coiling like serpents, or tall and straight as cathedral spires.

He lived in a one-roomed shack in the heart of a forest. In earlier years, when his wife had been alive, the candlemaker was happy; and, whenever the trees and shrubs that surrounded the cottage grew too high, together they would trim them down so that the sun could shine through the window and fill every corner of the little room with warmth and light.

But when his wife died, the old man forgot about the sunshine and let the forest grow high around his shack. The light could not penetrate the foliage that clung in great clusters to the walls and window. Even the door was overhung with ivy, and the candlemaker had to crouch

down to get in and out of his house. In the gloom he worked away, the only light coming from a corner, where a candle burned constantly beneath a picture of his wife. As the pale flame flickered on the glass, he imagined the reflected light was a smile dancing on her lips, playing in her eyes.

How he longed for the days when they first met! She was so young and fresh, earth brown curls brushing her cheeks and tumbling over her shoulders. Tears trickled down his face and fell into the bowls of wax he was working with. They had no children, so the only thing he could remember her by was the picture hanging peacefully in the corner.

One morning he awoke to find a glittering web of ice woven across his window pane. The sleeping stillness of snow falling on snow surrounded the shack and the green forest firs were cloaked in white. Winter had come.

"Soon it will be New Year," he thought. "I will make a very special New Year candle to burn below my dear wife's picture. It will have many flames and will be shaped like a tree."

For days and long nights the old man worked at the candle. He was still a fine craftsman. But few people bought his candles now, for he rarely set foot outside his home. He no longer walked to the village to sell his wares on market day. Soon everyone would forget him. Even so, he worked hard and his room was crowded with candles that nobody came to buy. He did not have money for fuel, nor was he strong enough to chop his own kindling from the forest. All winter he sat at his workbench, shivering in the icy gloom.

On Hogmanay, the last night of the Old Year, the candle was finished. He placed it beneath his wife's portrait.

"I shall light it when the clock strikes midnight," he decided.

It was still early evening. The candlemaker sat huddled in the big armchair, shrouded by a threadbare rug. The wind had dropped and all that could be heard was the silence of falling snow.

Suddenly he turned his head towards the door. What was that? Footsteps padding through the snow? It couldn't be — nobody ever visited him. Yet, there was the sound again! Slowly he raised his bent old body from the chair and opened the door. But no-one was there — only a bundle of fire-wood lying on the step.

"Who could have brought this?" he wondered, carrying his present inside. He lit a fire and soon his head was nodding in the drowsy warmth.

It was nearly midnight and the embers were glowing low down in the grate. An owl screeched through the forest. The candlemaker woke with a start.

"Not long now till midnight," he murmured, glancing at the clock. "Better light the candle." He fumbled through his pockets to find his last box of matches empty.

"Light the new candle with the old," he told himself. "Kindle the New Year with the Old."

And slowly the candle began to glow. There were seven flames, one at the tip of each branch of the waxen tree. As he lit the seventh, the clock struck twelve and the whole tree burst into flame. A strange white spirit leaped up from the blaze.

"Old man," she said to the candlemaker, who was trembling with fear. "I am the spirit of this beautiful tree you have made. The tears you wept into the wax created me. I am here to help you in your sorrow — my gift to you is youth." Her delicate hands quivered; she seemed to be clasping a flame.

"Look!" she called, and his eyes followed the graceful movement of her snow-white arms, as she thrust the flame into the middle of the room. "There is youth. Treat it dearly, for when the flames of my candle take their last breath and burn out, this youth will also die."

With these words she vanished. The fire that had surrounded her diminished, until only the seven flames of the seven branches were left flickering faintly.

The old man turned to look at the tongue of fire the spirit had cast into the middle of the room. It burned brilliantly, and grew higher until its tip almost licked the wooden rafters. The candlemaker recoiled in terror. Some invisible sculptor was moulding the flame into a human form. A moment later a beautiful youth stood before him. He was strangely like the old man's wife, but his hair was darker and his eyes smouldered rather than sparkled. His limbs were slender and strong as young saplings.

"Father, dear Father," he whispered. And he embraced the old man.

From that day, the candlemaker and the youth lived together in the shack. No longer did the old man weep when he thought of his wife — now he could even laugh with the memories.

That winter was hard and long. The old man passed the time teaching the youth to make candles. He was quick to learn and became very skilled at his work. The two would spend hours bent over the bowls of wax, while the clock ticked and the seven flames burned in the corner. The candlemaker was happy with his new son.

"A great spirit has given me this wonderful gift, and I must not lose it,' he thought. Indeed, he loved the youth so much that he was afraid of taking him out into the forest.

"If he hears the laughter of children from the village, and discovers the green trees and wild flowers, feels the sunshine warming his body, surely he will want to leave this old shack and travel the wide world. How terrible that would be! I could not live without him."

The old man determined never to let his son step outside the cottage. He locked the door and wore the key on a string around his neck.

"Father," the youth often asked, "what is beyond the door of our home?"

"A cruel and dangerous world, my son, a cruel and dangerous world."

But one morning, very early, while the old man and his son lay sleeping in their beds, a bird flew onto the highest branch of the tallest tree and sang a song that echoed right across the forest. The youth awoke.

"What is that sound?" he wondered. "Perhaps I was dreaming."

But a tiny patch of yellow sunlight had squeezed through the thick foliage that covered the window, and was dancing on the dusty floorboards. The pure spring air wafted under the door and filled the cottage with the fragrance of woodland moss.

"What a lovely smell!" exclaimed the youth. "What can it be? Father says the world outside is cruel, but perhaps if I only peeped it would do no harm."

He slipped out of bed and stole across the room to the workbench. He lifted his knife. Quietly he crept to the candlemaker's bedside. The old man lay in a deep sleep. The key, resting just above his heart, rose and fell with every breath. Candlemaking had taught the youth to be light of touch; in one swift movement he cut the string and held the key.

As the door creaked open, a thin ray of light filtered into the room through the curtain of leaves. Suddenly he was drenched in a shower

of morning sunshine. What a sight lay before those dark, wondering eyes! The trees had cast their cloaks of winter white, and wore green gowns of spring. In their cool shadows the grass was starred with flowers, rainbow-petalled heads nodding in the breeze. Birds sat on tree-tops, beaks thrust skyward, as they chorused their welcome to the day.

"Never have I seen or even dreamed of such a place," whispered the youth. "Why does my father despise it? Perhaps he has never seen the beauty that surrounds our cottage. I will wake him."

But the candlemaker was already stirring, for the sunlight had danced over his pillow, disturbing his sleep. He sat up and rubbed his eyes.

"Where has all this light come from?" he muttered. Then he saw his son in the doorway. "What are you doing!" he cried. "I told you never to open the door and you have defied me!"

"Father," replied the youth gently, trying to soothe the old man's temper. "Don't you know what it's like outside? Come, let me show you."

As the youth spoke, the old man glanced across the room to where the candle stood. The seven flames quivered like seven frightened souls and the wax dripped rapidly.

"Come inside!" shouted the candlemaker. "Come inside!" He seized his son by the arm, dragged him into the cottage and slammed the door, shutting out the light again. But the youth's body went limp in the old man's grasp.

"Open the door, Father!" he pleaded. "Open the door!" His voice grew faint and the fire that burned in his dark eyes began to fade. Waxen tears flowed down his paling cheeks.

The seven flames had gone out and the youth was no longer there. All that remained was a pool of wax at the candlemaker's feet. In desperation he rushed to the hearth. He picked up a piece of kindling and thrust it into the dying embers.

"My son will come back if I relight the candle," he told himself. "The draught as I shut the door must have blown it out."

But before he had taken his next breath, the seven wicks burst into flame, and once again he saw the spirit rise. She gazed at him knowingly and her voice was full of regret.

"I warned you, candlemaker. I warned you to treasure the youth dearly. But you were too afraid of losing him. You should have let him roam free as the wind, for youth will not be imprisoned." With these words the spirit vanished forever and the flames died away.

Many a time he tried to light the candle, but the wicks would not burn, and he became sadder than ever, not even bothering to work any more.

Summer passed, and winter; not a single light brightened the dark corners of the shack.

One morning the old man heard a lark singing far off in the forest.

"It must be Spring again," he sighed. "The Spring only brings sorrow, for she took my son away."

All of a sudden there was a knock on the door. He raised his head and lifted his weary body from the chair. He hobbled across the room and opened the door.

A child stood on the step. She smiled up at him, offering a small bunch of flowers.

"These are snowdrops," she said, "the first flowers of spring. I brought you the logs that cold Hogmanay. I live in the village. They told me you make candles. Can I see them?"

"Yes, yes .... candles, so many candles," murmured the old man, surprised and confused by his visitor.

He stood in the doorway, looking down at her for a long time. Her face was as bright as the snowdrops she held out to him, her eyes dark violets he had seen in the woods long ago.

At last he spoke: "You are the first flower of Spring; I have missed so many seasons in my foolish misery."

Taking her hand, he led her into his cottage. She gasped in wonder at the sight of so many candles.

"Let's light some!" she cried. "It's so dark in here."

"But I have no matches," he replied.

"I'll bring some from the village," she said. "I can fetch them now!"

"We'll do that later," said the candlemaker, picking her up in his arms and laughing. "But now, will you help me to cut down all the bushes and trees around my cottage?"

And soon the sunlight was pouring into his home again.

Princess Sorroway-over-the-Sea

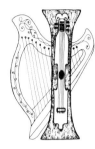 N A LAND across the sea, there was a garden. In the middle of this garden stood the statue of a princess. Her body was as still and cold as the white marble from which it had been sculpted. Her mouth was closed, as though it had never spoken, and her stone eyes gazed with motionless calm. She held a small harp. One hand touched the strings, but the stillness of those fingers seemed to silence all music forever.

Her name was Princess Sorroway-over-the-Sea.

The garden wasn't like a princess's garden at all. There were no flowers or lakes with swans and golden fish. Grass and trees alone grew there. When the wind blew, the grass swayed and sang a song, making music with the rustling leaves. Princess Sorroway-over-the-Sea listened. But no-one else ever heard the music, for a wall surrounded the garden, and the sound was too faint to be carried over its great height.

Many years ago, and so far away in time that no-one can remember, a king ruled this land. The queen had died while giving birth to their only child. This little girl was the king's most cherished possession.

On her seventh birthday the king took his daughter to visit his musical instrument maker, one of the finest craftsmen in the land. At the royal request a harp was fashioned, small enough for her infant hands to hold, and soon she had learned to compose her own melodies on the silver strings. She loved to wander along the sea-shore with her harp, listening to the ocean's dark song, until her fingers stirred in response, tracing rippling echoes of accompaniment to the waves.

"Princess Sorroway-over-the-Sea, that is the name they gave to me," were the words she sang.

PRINCESS
SORROWAY~
OVER-THE-
SEA

One day the princess did not return from her walk by the shore. The king's servants were sent out to search for her, boats put to sea, but she was not found. Several days later, the waves washed a small harp ashore, telling of her cruel fate.

In memory of his drowned daughter the king built a garden. Within its high wall he placed a marble statue of the little princess, her own words, "Princess Sorroway-over-the-Sea" carved on the pedestal. The gate was locked, and the key given to the king's gardener.

The faintest echo of birdsong, a note from a distant violin, a hint of music when a breeze strayed through the forest, all these were painful reminders to the king of his beloved daughter. "I will have my revenge!" he cried. And he issued an edict:

All the musical instruments in his kingdom were to be thrown into the sea.

Royal servants broke into houses and schools throughout the land, where children were busy at their music lessons, and seized the precious instruments from their hands. The workshops of every musical instrument maker were plundered. A shepherd broke a branch from a tree, and sat down in the sunshine to carve a whistle, only to have it snatched from his grasp as he blew his first tune.

But this hounding and destruction did not satisfy the king. He knew that music was still in the air when the wind blew through meadows and forests. So every blade of grass and every tree was cut down. Birds could find nowhere to nest and fled with their songs to foreign lands.

Silence reigned, and the king's despair drenched the heart of his people. Not a note of music could be heard. He was satisfied.

Many years passed. The king grew old and died. The people had long since forgotten the meaning of music. They still chopped down trees, cut the grass, and if a lost fragment of song found its passage into the world again through a child's voice, the adults quickly cried, "Ssh!" — though they couldn't remember why.

Long ago the king's gardener had died, and buried with him was the knowledge of what lay behind the garden wall. The gate was locked. No-one ever saw the statue of Princess Sorroway-Over-the Sea, standing in the wilderness that grew there, listening secretly to the song of the grass.

But she wasn't alone in her solitude. There was a little boy.

Every morning his parents hurried off to work, leaving him in the house. All day he played with his toys and books. Often he would sit down on the floor and cry. Everything was so quiet.

"Why don't you speak to me?" he shouted at his dolls. But their lips never moved.

One day, when he was wandering around the house, he found his way into the attic, and discovered a big wooden chest standing there. The hinges creaked as he lifted the heavy lid. To his disappointment he found that it was almost empty, with only a large rusty key and a brown paper bundle in one corner. Putting the key in his pocket, he reached for the package and untied the string. From the dusty paper, a mass of silver hair cascaded like a waterfall.

"Lovely!" he whispered, stroking the silver softness. "I wonder what it is?"

When his mother came home from work he showed her his treasures.

"This is your grandmother's hair," she told him.

"Why did she cut if off?" he asked.

"When your Granny was very old," his mother explained, "she became ill and had to stay in bed. She always complained that the brush made a terrible sound when I pulled it through her hair — I plaited her hair every morning. At last I had to cut it off. It seemed a shame to throw it away — such a pretty colour. So I kept it in the attic.

"And that old key was given to your Granny by her great-grandfather, who was the royal gardener, when this country had a king."

That night the little boy could not sleep. The moon shone on his face as he lay in bed remembering all that his mother had told him. After a while he sat up. He slipped his hand under the pillow and took out the brown paper package.

"The moon gleams like my grandmother's hair".

With this thought he climbed out of bed, crossed to the window and held the shining hair up to the moon. It glistened in the white light, brighter than a host of moonbeams. A breeze whispered through the window and the silver hair sighed.

"What a lovely sound!" cried the boy. "Let me hear it again!"

He listened. Once more the breeze came sighing through the window and the silver hair whispered. He tried to make the sound with his own lips, and soon he was singing.

The next day, when his parents had gone to work, he left home, clutching his brown paper bundle, the key tucked safely in his pocket.

"I must show my grandmother's hair to everyone. The sound will make them happy," he thought. But no-one wanted to listen. The old people especially grew agitated.

"Ssh!" they silenced him, and their eyes spoke of a distant fear.

"I shall find someone," the little boy told himself. "Surely someone will listen."

So he walked on and on. The sun sank down under the sea, and night filled the sky. On and on he walked but suddenly he stopped.

"What is that I hear?" he wondered, and followed the sound until he came to a high wall. It was clear now and rang through the night as though all the rivers in the world were singing together. He ran round

the wall and came to a gate. It was locked. But already his hand was searching through his pocket for the key — in an instant he knew this was the door it would unlock. He heard rust grind in the hole as the key turned, and with a drumming heart he pushed the gate open.

The garden was draped in a sheet of moonlight, and where the statue had been, the pedestal lay bare. Swaying trees stood out against the night sky like giants waving great arms at him. Long grass whispered secrets around the feet of Princess Sorroway-over-the-Sea, who walked towards him, plucking the strings of her harp and singing:

"Princess Sorroway-over-the-Sea
That is the name they gave to me;
Princess Sorroway-over-the-Sea,
At last, my friend, you have come to me."

She took the boy by the hand and told him to break a branch from a tree. Then she showed him how to tie his grandmother's hair around the branch to make a harp like her own. He plucked the shining strings and sang.

Princess Sorroway-over-the-Sea led him out of the garden. Singing and playing their harps they walked down a winding road to the sea.

"Princess Sorroway-over-the-Sea,
That is who I will always be;
Far away, far away, deep in the sea,
That is where I am longing to be.

Farewell, my friend, too long I have stayed,
Farewell, my friend, now don't be afraid;
With you harp and your voice fill the silence with sound,
Show all our people the joy you have found.

Princess Sorroway-over-the-Sea,
My home is waiting, now calling for me;
Far away, far away, deep in the sea,
That is where I am longing to be."

Singing these words, she waved to the boy and walked over the sand towards the sea. Deeper and deeper into the sea she walked, further and further away. The boy watched until she was only a tiny speck of moonlight on the waves.

Then up the winding road he walked, singing and playing his harp. On and on he walked, filling the air with music. Daylight was creeping into the night sky. One by one the windows of all the houses in the land were flung wide open.

One by one the people listened, and one by one they began to sing.

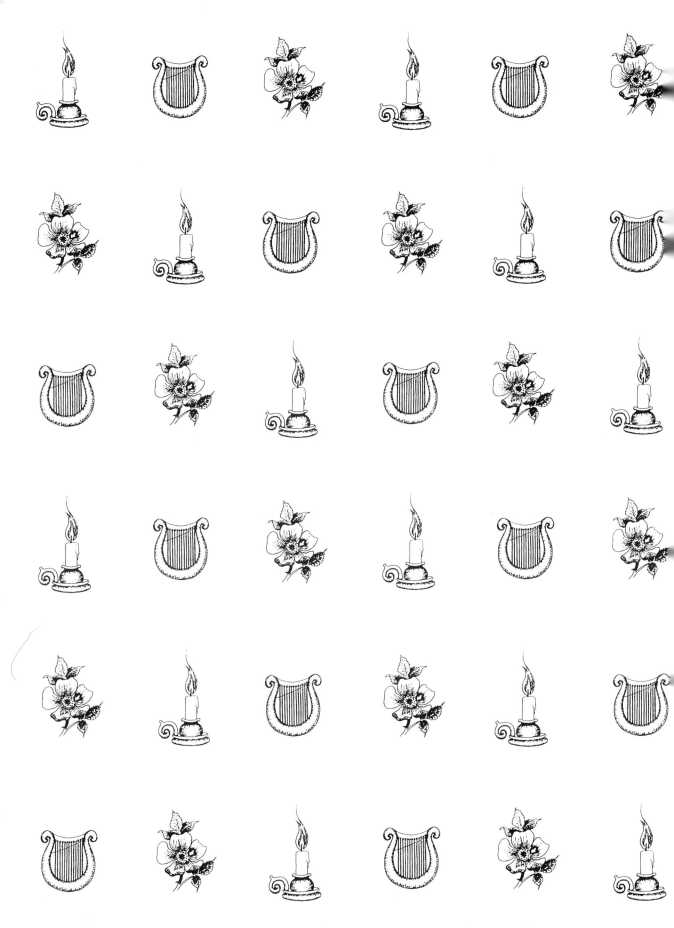